*For my sisters, Meghan and Natalie, who fill my
life with much love and laughter. - A.B.H.*

For Tom, who lights up my dreams. - B.H.

Text copyright © 2006 by Ashley Brooke Hornsby
Illustrations © 2006 Barbara Hranilovich

Glo E ™ is a trademark of Cepia LLC.

A CEPIA LLC BOOK

Published in the United States of America by Cepia LLC., Saint Louis Missouri
www.glo-e.com

ISBN 0-9777241-3-1
Printed in China

Pretty Little Lilly
and the
Land of Sweet Dreams

Written By:
Ashley Hornsby

Illustrated By:
Barbara Hranilovich

Pretty Little Lilly snuggled up tight in her bed once again,
Ready for her next dreamlike adventure to begin.
Her Mama tucked her in tight and turned out the light,
"Sweet dreams, my Pretty Little Lilly, I love you.
Goodnight."

Lilly sat alone in her room,
Looking up at the great big moon.
She snuggled up close to her sweet Glo E bear,
Waiting for the magical night they would share.

She closed her eyes
And was swept far far away
To the Land of Northern Lights
Where she and Glo E would play.
They crossed the colorful River of Lights,
The colors swirled and twirled
And rippled with delight.

They chased shooting stars, so vivid and bright,
Surrounded by fluffy clouds filled with light.
They slid down a magical and sparkling moonbeam,
To a place that was called the Land of Sweet Dreams.

This land was kissed by an early sunrise,
And with every little step there was a new surprise.
There were fields of soft flowers dripping with dew,
And clouds like cotton candy with a soft pink hue.
This field led to a forest filled with blossoming trees
With thousands of flowers and big beautiful leaves.
The forest lit up with a twinkling light,
It was indeed the most beautiful sight.

Lilly asked Glo E, "Where are we now?"

"Where sweet dreams are made special
And I'll show you how.
This is the place where fairies play;
They dance and sing and dream all day.
It's a little bit past the Land of Northern Lights,
And only a dream or two to the right.
These fairies are special, you should probably know,
They sparkle and twinkle, shine, glitter and glow.
Sparkle fairies are the givers of dreams,
And only the sweet ones it would seem."

Lilly looked around with wonder and awe,
Amazed by the twinkling sparkles she saw.
They twinkled in silver, they glittered in green,
They sparkled in colors only seen in sweet dreams.
Hundreds of fairies were dancing around,
Sparkling and twinkling to a magical sound.

Far in the distance Lilly heard a faint cry.
It was then all the fairies sang a sweet lullaby.
The words had no reason; the words had no rhyme,
But everything grew so peaceful at this point in time.
As the fairies sang sweetly their sparkles shone bright,
Then there was a swirling and twirling beautiful light.

The light was soft, warm and sweet,
Changing colors to the lullaby's soothing beat.
A few moments longer the crying was gone
And that was the end of the beautiful song.
The fairies continued to giggle and play
As if this sort of thing happened every single day.

Lilly asked Glo E
About the fairies' song,
And Glo E explained,
"It was for a dream
that went wrong.
These fairies make dreams
Magical and fun,
But once in a while
There can be a bad one.
Whenever they hear a little cry
These sweet little fairies
Sing that sweet lullaby.
They call it 'The Song
For the Dream That Went Wrong.'
They sing and they sing
Until the cry goes away,
Until they know that
The child's dream is okay."

Lilly said, "What if *I* have
A dream that goes wrong?"

"Then the fairies," said Glo E,
"Would sing you that sweet little song.
You would feel a warm and beautiful light,
A glistening glow that would calm the night.
They would sparkle and twinkle and hold your hand
And bring you to this sweet dreamlike land."

As Glo E spoke, the words became real,
With a warm sparkling light that Lilly could feel.
She was surrounded by thousands of little twinkling lights
That sparkled and shone as the sky turned to night.

She lay down in the flowers, once dripping with dew,
And the cotton candy clouds now had a purple hue.
As nighttime blanketed this Sweet Dream Land,
Glo E held Lilly's sweet little hand.
It was now time for the fairies to sleep tight,
And time for Pretty Little Lilly to awake from the night.

Lilly awoke and the fairies were gone,
But she'd always remember that beautiful song.
Her room was bathed with the warm morning sunlight,
And out of the corner of her eye she saw a twinkling light.
Pretty Little Lilly smiled and hugged her sweet Glo E bear,
Waiting for the next dream they soon would share.